Pups

FRAMED!

Mystery Pups

FRAMED!

by Jodie Mellor
Illustrated by Penny Dann

SIMON AND SCHUSTER

SIMON AND SCHUSTER
First published in Great Britain in 2008 by Simon and Schuster UK Ltd
A CBS COMPANY

Simon & Schuster UK Ltd
Africa House, 64-78 Kingsway, London WC2B 6AH.

A CIP catalogue record for this book is available from the British Library.

ISBN: 978-1-84738-225-2

Printed and bound in Great Britain
by CPI Cox and Wyman, Reading, Berkshire RG1 8EX

www.simonsays.co.uk

CHAPTER ONE

"Caitlin, wake up – Megan and Lauren are here!"

From under the covers of her warm bed, Caitlin heard her mum call.

"Time to get up!" Caitlin's friend Lauren yelled as she sprinted upstairs.

Megan stayed downstairs in the hallway to keep an eye on Buster and Dylan. "Sit!" she told the two pups sternly.

Buster, the cute pale brown mongrel, and Dylan, the sleek black Labrador, sat. They gazed up at Megan, tails swishing gently over the shiny floor.

Upstairs, Lauren charged into Caitlin's bedroom

and dragged back the covers. "Get up, lazy bones. It's nine o'clock!"

Caitlin tried to pull the duvet back up over her head.

"Get up!" Lauren repeated, sitting on the bed and jiggling up and down. "Today's the day for our second Puppy Club meeting. You need to get up and bring Daisy to Megan's house."

Caitlin sat up straight. "Wow, yes, I forgot!" she said. "We're going to do the Puppy Club promises again, and give the pups their medallions!"

"Exactly!" Lauren's brown eyes shone. "And we'll wear our Puppy Club badges, just like last time…"

Caitlin jumped out of bed and scrambled into her jeans and a pale blue sweatshirt, stuffed her feet into a pair of trainers, tucked her toy pup Daisy under her arm, then dashed downstairs to join the others.

"No time for breakfast!" Caitlin called to her mum, as she, Lauren and Megan shot out of the front door. "Bye!"

The Magic Mountain Puppy Club was on the move, heading for Megan's place, rushing full-tilt towards another super-sleuth adventure.

"We are members of the Magic Mountain Puppy Club." With serious faces, Lauren, Caitlin and Megan read out their promises.

Bouncy Buster, cute Daisy and clever Dylan stared eagerly at the gold medallions which the girls held in their hands.

"Where's your badge?" Megan whispered to Caitlin.

"Here!" Caitlin replied, pushing back her long hair to reveal her Puppy Club Members' badge.

"Just checking!" Megan muttered, satisfied that she, Caitlin and Lauren were all wearing their badges.

"We promise to feed our puppies and play with them," they chanted. "We promise to take them for long walks."

The sun shone down on the pups and their owners. Dylan and Buster's tails wagged. Daisy's eyes sparkled in the bright light.

Then Lauren, Megan and Caitlin leant forward and hung the magic gold medallions around their puppies' necks.

The girls waited for something to happen.

Lauren sighed and shook her head. "I don't feel dizzy like last time!"

"Me neither," a disappointed Megan agreed.

But Caitlin had been staring at Daisy and
was sure one ear had moved. "Look – Daisy's
coming alive!" she whispered.

Then, as the puppies' medallions glinted in the
sun, Lauren felt the lawn start to tilt and turn,
and Megan saw the green trees blur and spin.

"*Now* I'm dizzy!" Lauren cried.

Whizz! The world tilted and turned like a ride at the fairground. The girls seemed to float up from the ground then spin and spin towards a brilliant white light.

"Wow, it's happening!" Megan gasped.

Buster, Dylan and Daisy bounded ahead into the centre of the light.

"Yippee – Daisy's come back to life!" Caitlin rushed after her magical pup and was lost in the dazzle.

"Wait for us!" Lauren begged, as the three Mystery Pups led her, Megan and Caitlin into a magical world.

CHAPTER TWO

Zap! Lauren, Caitlin and Megan made a hard landing. They hit the ground running, five metres behind Buster, Daisy and Dylan, who raced ahead across a dimly-lit hallway.

"This is Sleuth City by Night, playing mellow music to snooze to," a voice on the radio schmoozed as the Mystery Pups charged through an open door into the biggest, grandest living room the girls had ever seen.

There were three cream leather sofas and a huge crimson rug in the middle of a marble floor. Six gleaming glass chandeliers hung from the ceiling, and the walls were crammed with paintings framed in gold.

"Who lives here?" Caitlin asked, her mouth open in amazement.

"Someone mega-rich," Megan pointed out.

"Whoa!" Lauren cried, as Buster bashed against a table leg and made a lamp wobble. She rushed to catch it before it toppled to the floor. "That was close!"

"Yip!" Daisy barked, running up to Caitlin.

"What is it? What do you want?" Caitlin asked. *And why are we here?*

"Take a look at this place!" Megan said to Lauren and Caitlin. "It's crammed with … stuff!"

"Maybe it's a museum," Lauren suggested as she circled a marble statue.

But Megan spotted two half-empty wine glasses on one of the tables and a pair of red high heeled shoes under a sofa. "No. Someone lives here."

Dylan darted under the sofa and grabbed a red shoe. He brought it straight to Megan and dropped it at her feet.

"You want me to find who this belongs to?" she asked him thoughtfully.

"Yap!" Then, *sniff-sniff, snuffle-snuffle* – Dylan trotted towards a stairway at the far side of the room.

"Hey!" Lauren's voice brought the girls and the pups running. They gathered by the marble fireplace, staring up at the wall. "Look!" Lauren whispered, pointing to the empty space above the mantelpiece.

"There should be another picture there!" Megan said slowly. "The wallpaper has faded everywhere except here."

"Someone took it down. Maybe it needed cleaning," Caitlin guessed.

"Yip-yip-yap-yap!" The three pups barked and jumped up against the fireplace.

"Or maybe someone broke in and stole it!" exclaimed Lauren.

"Yip-yip-yip!"

"Dylan, Daisy, Buster - ssshhh!" Caitlin, Megan and Lauren raised their fingers to their lips.

"And here is some breaking news from Sleuth City Police Department." The radio announcer broke through the singer's fading warble. "We're getting reports of a major art theft from the luxury apartment of rock legend Jimmi Diamond."

Megan, Caitlin and Lauren's eyes almost popped out of their heads as they stared at the empty wall above the fireplace. "That's where we are - right here, right now!" Caitlin gasped, spotting a diamond-studded guitar in the corner.

"According to early police reports, thieves broke into the Diamonds' apartment in central Sleuth City earlier tonight. They made off with a masterpiece by French artist, Claude Rosier. The portrait was recently valued at a cool five million! Now that, guys and girls, is enough cash to wake every one of us from our beauty sleep!"

Megan swallowed hard. If the police caught the girls and their pups in the Diamonds' apartment, they'd be in real trouble.

Caitlin scooped little Daisy up from the floor. "Uh-oh, we need to get out!" she whispered.

Lauren turned to see if she could spot the exit. "We so-o-o do!" she agreed.

Suddenly the dim lights turned bright and an alarm shattered the silence. "Too late!" Megan and Caitlin groaned.

Buster jumped up and tugged at Lauren's T-shirt. Clever Dylan trotted to a bookcase behind a sofa then gave a high yelp.

Just in time, Megan, Caitlin and Daisy, Lauren and Buster ran for cover. They dived behind the sofa then into the gap under the bookcase.

Weird, thought Megan. *Why should the alarm go off right now?*

Lauren was picturing policemen dragging them out of their hiding place, asking them questions about the theft which they wouldn't be able to answer. "How did you get into the apartment? Where's the painting? Come on, spill the beans!"

"Try not to breathe," Caitlin warned, peering out and wondering what had happened to

Jimmi Diamond and the woman who owned the red shoes.

The burglar alarm jangled on, sirens sounded in the street below and the gaping space above the fireplace screamed "Stop thief!" to all who saw it.

CHAPTER THREE

A buzzer sounded alongside the alarm and at last two people came down the glass stairs.

One was a tall, blonde woman dressed in a red silk dressing gown. The other was a man – smaller and older than the woman and wearing his thin grey hair in a ponytail. He walked to the door and pressed a button. A small screen lit up, showing the street scene below. "Who's there?" he asked.

"This is Agent Greene from the Police Department," the man on the screen answered.

"OK, come on up." The ponytail man pressed another button then turned to the woman. "They took their time," he muttered.

The woman checked her hair in a mirror, fluffing it up with her fingertips. "They're here now, Jimmi, and that's what matters."

From under the bookcase, Megan, Lauren and Caitlin listened hard. They held their breaths and prayed that the pups wouldn't give them away.

"Yip!" Daisy let out the smallest yelp and wriggled in Caitlin's arms. Luckily for them, at the same moment there was a knock on the main door of the apartment and Jimmi Diamond went to answer it. "Come right on in," he told Greene. "Man, are we glad to see you!"

"Try to stay calm, Mr Diamond," the cop said, scanning the room and spotting the empty space above the fireplace. "I have agents guarding the entrance to the building and a couple more posted on the street corner. If the thieves are still around, my men will get them."

"Thank goodness!" Helen Diamond sobbed, trembling and looking as if her legs were about to give way. She sat on the sofa closest to where the girls and the pups hid.

"Yip!" Daisy yelped again.

"Ssshhh!" Caitlin begged, holding her tight.

"Now, Sir." Turning to Jimmi D, the cop hooked his thumbs into his belt and gave the rock star a hard stare. "Do you know anyone who could be behind this theft? Any friend or tradesman who could have worked out how to fool the security system?"

Jimmi Diamond looked blank. "This came as a complete shock," he answered. "Look at Helen – you can see how hard she's taking it."

"Grrrr … !" Buster growled and looked as if he was about to break cover, until Lauren held him back.

"Such a beautiful painting!" Helen sobbed.

"And worth a fortune," Jimmi added with a frown.

Megan sat back deeper into the shadows. *It's a good job that alarm is drowning us out!* she thought. She pressed against the wall and to her surprise heard a *click*. Suddenly the bottom section of the bookcase swung open behind them.

"…Do you have a photograph of the painting?" Greene was asking Jimmi. "We'll show it to the TV boys. That way, everyone will know exactly what we're looking for."

"It's a portrait of the artist's wife, Fifi, and their dog, Pierrot," Jimmi replied.

"There's a photo in the office. Go find it for him, Helen."

Megan, Caitlin and Lauren glanced over their shoulders and saw that the secret door had opened into a dark passage.

"This is our chance!" Lauren exclaimed while the three pups sniffed around.

"...To get away without being seen!" Caitlin added.

"Wait!" Megan took one last listen before she closed the secret door.

"I want you to put this top of your list of major crimes," Jimmi Diamond was telling Agent Greene. "I invested more dough in that painting than most people earn in a lifetime..."

"Yessir!" Greene was replying. "Right at the top of my list, trust me!"

Click! Megan shut the door and the voices faded.

Inside the passage it was pitch black.

"Come on!" Lauren hissed.

"I bet this is how the robbers got in and out!"

Caitlin whispered as Buster and Daisy followed Dylan, sniffing and snuffling as they went.

"What's it for? Who builds a secret passage into an apartment?" Megan was trying to think things through as usual.

Suddenly Dylan stopped, and Daisy and Buster bundled into him.

"Uh-oh, here's another door!" Lauren's heart sank as she felt the smooth surface blocking their way.

"Is it locked?" Caitlin wanted to know.

"Yes." Lauren's fingertips ran over the door

from top to bottom. So far as she could make out there was no handle to turn, no lock to open.

"We're stuck," Megan gasped. "If there isn't a way out of here we'll have to turn around and go back!"

Meanwhile, Jimmi and Helen Diamond showed Agent Greene to the door of their apartment.

"We'll have this on the major News channel within the hour," Greene promised, waving the photo of Rosier's famous painting at them. "It's already been on the radio, but the TV will reach millions of viewers. We're not going to let this gang go free, believe me."

"Good." Nodding grimly, Jimmi closed the door after the tough policeman.

"Good," Helen echoed, walking back to her cream sofa and slipping her bare feet into the red shoes. Then she rested her head against a cushion.

Jimmi picked up a TV remote and flicked until he got the News. Then the two of them sat in silence … waiting.

CHAPTER FOUR

"We can't turn around and go back!" Lauren insisted as the girls shoved hard against the door. "There has to be a way out!"

Daisy wriggled in Caitlin's arms, while Dylan sniffed hard at the gap under the door.

But it was Buster who solved the problem. With a high leap against the door frame, the madcap mongrel reached a switch.

Click! His front paws flicked it and the passage was flooded with light.

"Good boy!" Lauren cried. "Now we can see what we're doing!"

"More buttons." Quietly Megan examined a

small metal panel. "There must be a lift behind here." She pressed one of the buttons.

Swish! The door slid open and the three pups bundled in, with the girls hard on their heels.

"Close the door – quick!" Caitlin gasped.

Lauren pressed another button. The lift began to rise quickly, up and up, to the very top of the tower block where it stopped with a shudder.

"Yap-yap-woof!" Buster, Daisy and Dylan were impatient for the door to open.

One more press and *swish!* – Caitlin, Megan and Lauren peered out across a vast, flat rooftop. A cool wind blew between water-storage tanks and satellite dishes. All around there was the orange glow of big city lights.

Caitlin followed Daisy as the little Yorkie dashed out of the lift and scampered towards the edge of the roof. She stopped with a gasp. "Wow, this building is seriously high!"

Megan and Lauren joined her to gaze down at the streets below. Cars were tiny and people

looked like small dots under the bright street lamps.

"OK, it looks like our pups have landed us with a big problem," Caitlin muttered, standing back from the edge. She didn't like heights – they made her legs wobble and her mouth go dry. "How are we supposed to help solve the crime if we're stuck up here on the roof with no way off?"

Lauren tried to figure it out. "So how does Jimmi Diamond get off the roof after he uses his secret lift?" she asked.

"He's rich. He probably has a helicopter." Quick-thinking Megan came up with the answer. She spotted a big yellow circle painted on the roof. "Think about it. He's mega-famous. If he goes in and out of the main door like everyone else in this building, people are always recognising him, even when he wants to be left alone."

"You mean, like his fans, plus TV cameras and stuff?" Lauren nodded.

"So this is his private heli-pad," Megan went on, pacing out the yellow circle and staring up at the night sky.

"I don't like it up here." Caitlin shivered in the cold wind. "I think we should go back down in the lift."

"Then what?" Lauren asked. "We'd be back where we started."

"No, listen, I've got a better idea," Megan interrupted. "All these tower blocks have fire escapes, don't they?"

"Yes!" Lauren began to search for a metal staircase down the side of the building. "Come on, Buster – let's find the stairs!"

Meanwhile, Dylan stood at the foot of a nearby pole and barked to bring Megan running.

"Uh-oh!" she muttered, staring up at a small square box. "Dylan just spotted a camera – you know, for security. It's filming us right now!"

"Yap!" Buster had found the stairs.

Daisy wriggled out of Caitlin's arms and ran to join him. "Let's go!" Caitlin gasped.

And without stopping to think, the girls and their pups were sprinting from the roof and clattering down the metal stairs – ten, twenty … fifty … Down and down until they almost reached the ground.

"Grrrr!" A deep growl greeted them from below and a dark shape barred their way.

CHAPTER FIVE

"Stop right there!" a man's voice cried.

Lauren, Caitlin and Megan stopped dead, but Dylan, Buster and Daisy dashed boldly on. Down the steps they raced until they came face to face with a guard dog.

"Grrrrr!" The black dog bared his teeth. He wore a leather collar with steel studs, and his chest was wide as a barrel.

"Yip!" Fearless Daisy darted straight at the enemy, scooting between his bowed front legs while Buster made a mighty leap. He soared clean over the guard dog and began snapping and biting at his heels.

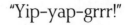

"Yip-yap-grrr!"

Then Dylan charged the big dog. He crouched low and dared him to attack. The heavyweight dog was too slow to stop Dylan, who swerved then grabbed the security guard's leg between his jaws.

"Quick!" Lauren said.

"Pesky little mutt!" the security guard grunted, trying in vain to shake Dylan off.

"Yip-yap!" Buster and Daisy charged the guard dog and confused him, running circles around him while the girls made their escape.

"This way!" Caitlin spotted an alley leading towards the bright street lights.

"We're with you!" Breathlessly, Lauren and

Megan followed. "Come on, Buster and Daisy! Come on, Dylan!"

The yellow, red and green lights of the street beckoned. The girls and the pups burst out of the alley.

The little gang were out on the sidewalk, weaving through the crowd. Behind them, the security guard and his dog were in hot pursuit.

"We've got to lose them for good!" Lauren cried, glancing over her shoulder.

Ahead there was a big square with a fountain. Though it was late, it was still jammed with cars and sightseers.

"Water!" Megan gasped. She took the lead and made for the square. They were gaining ground on their pursuers, losing themselves in the crowd. Now Megan was sure that they couldn't be seen.

"What's with the water?" Lauren wondered. She soon found out.

The girls and pups pushed their way

towards the fountain. A jet of water rose high in the air then splashed back down into a pool. Still leading, Megan climbed on to the low wall surrounding the fountain. "Ready?" she asked.

Dylan, Daisy and Buster woofed and wagged their tails.

Lauren and Caitlin stood on the brink and took deep breaths.

"Where did those kids go?" the security

guard yelled from the edge of the square.

"Go!" Megan cried.

And the three girls jumped.

Splash!

Megan, Lauren and Caitlin plunged into the fountain. The pups yelped and jumped after them.

Cold water showered over their heads as they waded across the pool.

"Why?" Lauren demanded as they struggled

out at the far side. She was shivering and dripping.

Dylan, Daisy and Buster climbed out of the fountain and shook themselves.

"Because we'd lost them in the crowd and dogs can't follow a trail through water!" Megan pointed out.

Sure enough, the guard dog had come to a halt by the far side of the fountain. He was sniffing and going round in circles, while his owner lost his cool. "I'll lose my job over this!" he told strangers in the square. "My boss said to stop those kids or else!"

But the girls and their pups were already long gone.

They made their way to Sleuth City Central Park, where they found a summer house and decided to bed down for the night.

Lauren sighed. "That stolen painting had better be worth all this trouble!"

"Because Jimmi Diamond and his wife definitely aren't," Caitlin added. "I mean – they let that guard dog loose on us!"

"Yes, but it's their painting that went missing, and it's them we're supposed to help," Megan argued.

There was a longer silence then Caitlin said, "I wish Daisy could talk. She'd know what to do next."

"So would Dylan," Megan added.

"And Buster." Lauren made sure that they

included her own ace-detective pup.

But right now all three snoozed and snored. Now and again an ear twitched and a tail wagged dreamily.

Before they knew it, Caitlin, Lauren and Megan were fast asleep.

CHAPTER SIX

Sleuth City woke early. Before dawn, trucks drove through the streets to collect bags of rubbish and sweep the sidewalks. By 7am, breakfast bars had opened to serve office workers as they made their way to the subway.

"I'm stiff!" Caitlin sighed, waking up beside Daisy and stretching.

"Ouch!" Megan's arm had cramp.

"Time to get up!" Lauren called from the summer house door. She was up before the others and had let the pups out. "Come on, rise and shine!"

'Major Art Theft!' 'Private Collector Loses

Priceless Portrait!' Out on the main street, the break-in was already big news.

Megan, Caitlin and Lauren stopped to read the headlines. Their puppies stayed obediently to heel.

'Jimmi D Painting Stolen!' People bought the paper and read the story on their way to work. They sat at breakfast bars, discussing the theft.

"It's hard to feel sorry for a guy with that kind of money," they grumbled.

But others were on the rock star's side. "Jimmi Diamond makes great music," they argued. "He deserves his success and the money that comes with it."

Megan sidled up to a woman outside a coffee bar who was reading to her neighbour. "Police investigators are checking out an early lead involving Tom Drake, Diamond's ex-manager." She listened in while Caitlin and Lauren watched the TV screen above the bar, hoping for more news.

"The split between Diamond and Drake took place earlier this year, with Drake claiming that he is still owed millions by Diamond," the woman read on.

"No wonder the cops are on Drake's tail," the man drinking coffee next to the woman said. "That looks like a pretty strong motive to break in and steal the picture if you ask me."

The woman shrugged and pushed the newspaper aside. "I've got to get to work." She slid from her stool and left.

Megan seized the crumpled newspaper then went to join Megan and Caitlin. "Anything on the TV?" she asked.

"More of this stuff about the ex-agent," Caitlin told her. "Since the split with Jimmi Diamond, Tom Drake and his family have had to move out of the apartment next to Jimmi D's place."

"Because Tom Drake is broke – no money

left – zilch!" Megan cut in. "He's been telling people that he'll find a way to get his own back against Jimmi…"

"Wait!" It was Caitlin's turn to interrupt. She pointed to the TV screen high on the wall. "There's more!"

On the screen a blonde woman faced the camera. "Breaking news on the Rosier theft!" she announced. "Police have issued a warrant for

the arrest of Tom Drake. His last known address is in Linford on the west side of Sleuth City."

"Linford," Lauren muttered, making sure she remembered the name.

"We're out of here!" Lauren whispered to Megan and Caitlin, dashing back on to the street to gather up the pups who had been waiting patiently.

"Where to?" Caitlin asked. She picked Daisy

up, out of the way of trampling feet and swishing car tyres.

"Linford, of course!" Lauren stooped to give Buster a pat.

"To find Tom Drake," Megan added. Smart Dylan looked up at her as if he understood every word. He stood up and wagged his tail.

"Woof!" Dylan said, trotting off down the street.

CHAPTER SEVEN

Down in the subway, the girls studied the map on the wall.

"Here's Linford," Megan traced the route with her finger. "We have to cross the river and get off five stops from here."

In the crush of the rush hour, the girls and the pups squeezed on to an underground train. They rode shoulder to shoulder, carefully carrying Dylan, Buster and Daisy.

"Cute pups!" A fellow passenger smiled.

"This is our stop!" Lauren announced. She and Buster were the first to leave the carriage and find the escalator to ground level.

They went up on the moving stairway until they came out of Linford station. Concrete tower blocks rose on either side, but they were dull and drab compared with the glitzy buildings in central Sleuth City.

Caitlin took one look around and held on tight to Daisy. Meanwhile, Megan took out her newspaper and re-read the front page. "I think I spotted a street name for Tom Drake in here," she muttered. "…Yes, here it is. It says he was forced to move to an old terraced house in Upper Dock Street."

"So we have an address." Caitlin was glad to move on. She read a street sign. "This is River Street. If we head downhill we should come to the river."

"And Dock Street should be down there somewhere," Megan agreed.

Together they set off down the shabby street, past drab fast-food places and low cost shops. When they came to the end, they saw a wide stretch of grey water lined with tall metal cranes. Across the river, the swish blocks of central Sleuth City glinted and gleamed.

"This must be the docks. And this sign says Lower Dock Street," Caitlin said, glancing left.

Already Buster and Dylan had made a right turn on to Upper Dock Street. *Sniff-snuffle.* They jumped puddles in the sidewalk, leading the girls past a long row of houses with faded doors. Rusty bikes leant against railings, a kid on a skateboard whizzed by.

"Yap!" Buster darted out of the way of the skateboarder – a boy in a baseball cap worn

back-to-front, with floppy fair hair over his eyes.

"Woof!" Dylan took one look and began to chase the boy down the street.

"Dylan, come back!" Megan called. "Leave him alone!"

But the little Labrador raced as fast as his short legs could carry him, barking at the skateboarder, who went even faster to get away.

And now Buster joined in, yapping loudly.

"What's up with them?" Caitlin asked, still clutching Daisy.

The girls began to run. The boy on the skateboard come to a kerb and overbalanced into the gutter.

"Hey!" the boy shouted angrily at the girls.

"Sorry!" Lauren dashed up and grabbed Buster around his belly. "They're not usually like this."

"Woof–woof–yap!"

"I'm out of here," the boy told them, setting his skateboard level on the ground.

At last Caitlin arrived with Daisy. "Wait a second," she said to the boy. "We need to ask you something."

"No time, sorry." He began to skate away, the board rattling over the rough surface.

"Do you know where Tom Drake lives?" Caitlin yelled after him.

"Yip!" Daisy nodded.

The boy stopped dead. He jumped off his board and let it roll away into the gutter. "Who wants to know?" he said with a frown.

"We do. And so do the Sleuth City police." Caitlin ran forward. "Tom lives round here, doesn't he?"

The boy's frown deepened. "He didn't do anything wrong, whatever the cops think."

"How do you know Tom Drake wasn't the one who stole the painting?" Megan was still having trouble holding Dylan. She stared at the frowning boy.

Lauren joined in. "Do you know him?"

"You could say that." The boy blushed then owned up. "Actually, he's my dad."

"Your dad!" Caitlin, Lauren and Megan gasped. The kid held his head high. "My name's Josh Drake," he told them. "And anyone who calls Tom Drake a thief is a liar!"

CHAPTER EIGHT

"I hear you!" Caitlin told Josh. She for one believed him.

"Dad never stole anything in his whole life!" Josh insisted. "He was at home with Mom and me all last night. We watched TV then went to bed – end of story."

Standing outside a boarded-up shop, with Dylan and Buster scouting ahead, the girls listened to Josh's account of what had happened.

"Are you sure your dad didn't slip out late at night?" Lauren asked.

"No way. He wouldn't do that." Josh's answer was firm.

"But isn't it true that your dad and Jimmi Diamond had a big fight over money?" Megan checked. "That would give him a reason to steal the picture and try to get his own back, wouldn't it?"

Caitlin gave Megan a quick dig with her elbow. But the suspicious question had made Josh angry and he turned his back on them.

"I'm out of here – for sure!" he muttered.

"No, wait!" Caitlin stood in his way. "I believe you, Josh. And so does Daisy!"

The little Yorkie stretched out to lick the boy's hand.

"You know the police are looking for your dad right now?" Caitlin said.

"Yeah, I heard the News. But Dad has a part-time job delivering bread for a bakery. I've been out looking for him. He probably doesn't even know the stupid painting has been stolen."

"When's he due home?" Megan wanted to know.

Along the street two police cars drew up outside a run-down terraced house.

"Soon. He might be back already," Josh answered. Then he spotted the cars. "Oh no – now I'm too late to warn him!"

Panicking, Josh started to run towards the first police car. He pushed past two burly policemen and shouted ahead to his house. "Run, Dad! Don't let them get you!"

The noise brought people to the doors of their houses and shops.

"Cut it out!" Agent Greene grabbed hold of Josh. He motioned for his two uniformed men to get inside Drake's house and make their arrest.

Just then, a white delivery van turned a corner and slowly approached.

"That's Tom Drake's van!" Megan read the sign on the side – *Harvest Bread*. "And look, Buster and Dylan are trying to warn him!"

Sure enough, the two pups charged towards the tall, fair-haired man stepping down from the van. They circled him and barked their warning.

But the cops were quick. They were halfway up the stone steps to Drake's house, but now they turned and raced towards the dazed van driver.

"What is this?" Tom Drake had walked into a nightmare. Neighbours crowded the street, cops were running towards him.

"Run, Dad, run!" Josh yelled as Agent Greene held him back.

So Tom turned and ran. He vaulted a rubbish bin and nipped down an alley, then tried to lose the cops down a side passage.

Buster and Dylan guarded the entry to the alley as the cops approached.

But they were small – no match for the tough men, who brushed them aside. So the pups ran after them, trying to trip and hold them up as long as possible.

Tom Drake's heart thumped hard, he was out of breath and the cops were still coming after him. He turned another corner – and ran into a dead end!

"Gotcha!" The cops showed up just as Tom realised there was no way out. Though Dylan and Buster yapped at their heels, the cops got their man.

"You're arrested on suspicion of a major theft," they told Tom Drake.

"What?" Tom tried to wrestle free.

"We think you have something belonging to your old buddy, Jimmi Diamond – a little matter of a Rosier painting."

"No way! This can't be happening!" Tom struggled, but he had no chance against the two trained officers.

They handcuffed him and led him out of the alley into Dock Street.

Caitlin saw Josh's pale, shocked face as they put Tom Drake in the police car. "Don't worry – we'll help you," she promised quietly.

Josh didn't hear. He was staring at the orange flashing light on top of the cop car as it drove his dad away.

CHAPTER NINE

"Let us in," Caitlin pleaded at the door of Josh Drake's house. It was half an hour since the police had made their arrest.

Josh answered their knock. He looked at the three girls and their pups, then shook his head.

"What do you want? Do you *want* to make things even worse?"

He picked on Caitlin. "If it hadn't been for you, I could've warned Dad to run and he wouldn't have got himself arrested."

Caitlin sighed. "For some reason, the police need to talk to your dad. But maybe they'll just ask him a few questions then let him go."

"Or maybe not," Josh said angrily. He slumped against the wall, head down.

"I think you'd better leave," he muttered.

Just then Josh's mum came down the stairs saying she'd just taken a phone call from the police.

Everyone stopped dead. They could tell by Mrs Drake's shocked face that it wasn't good news.

"Josh, they just finished interviewing your dad over at the Central Police Department."

"And?"

Mrs Drake took a deep breath. "They've charged him with stealing Jimmi's painting. It looks like they're going to send him to jail and there isn't a thing we can do!"

"OK, let's work this out," Megan said.

The girls and pups were in the kitchen with Josh. Lucy Drake had gone back upstairs.

"Megan's the brainy one," Caitlin explained to Josh.

Megan turned to Lauren and spoke slowly. "I'm thinking about what exactly happened when we – erm – you know, 'landed' in the Diamond Tower."

"Yeah, how did you get in there?" Josh wanted to know. He'd already heard what Megan, Lauren and Caitlin had said about being at the scene when the cops first arrived and he was still sitting there, scratching his head over the whole thing.

"You don't want to know!" Lauren insisted. "Let's just say, it's down to the pups."

"They're … special!" Caitlin added brightly.

Dylan, Buster and Daisy lay under the kitchen table taking one of their naps. At the sound of his name, Buster opened one eye then closed it again.

Lauren pressed ahead. "What happened was, we heard the man on the radio say there was breaking news about a robbery…"

"But there was no sign of anyone in the apartment," Megan went on. "And when Jimmi Diamond and Helen did come downstairs, they were yawning and looking kind of bored."

"Yes. They didn't act like their house had just been burgled," Caitlin agreed. "Helen only got upset when the police came."

"That was weird." Megan frowned. "How well do you know Jimmi Diamond?" she asked Josh. "What's he like?"

Josh shrugged. "He's OK. I grew up around him because my dad worked for him all those years. Jimmi and Helen don't have kids, so she enjoyed doing stuff with me when I was younger. She'd take me to the park."

"But what's Jimmi like?" Megan insisted. "Is he one of those moody celebs?"

"I guess." Josh shrugged again. "Everyone around him does what he tells them. Nobody argues."

"And he's got money stashed away everywhere?" Lauren asked.

"He's loaded," Josh agreed. "But Dad says he's mean with his money. He wouldn't pay what he owed us – which is how we ended up here."

"That's tough," Caitlin murmured. "Would it make any difference now if you tried to talk to Jimmi?"

"Sounds like a good idea!" Lauren said.

Megan was more doubtful. "It would be good to get back into the apartment to take another look around, but from what I saw of Jimmi last night, I don't think it'll be that easy to talk to him."

"Yap-woof-yip!" Daisy, Dylan and Buster drowned her out with their barks.

"Wait here," Josh told the girls, running upstairs and coming down with a small plastic card. "This is an electronic pass into our old apartment. It's still vacant and it's right next door to Jimmi and Helen's place."

"Cool!" Megan liked the sound of this. "What's the quickest way back?"

"Over Linford Bridge," Josh answered, grabbing his cap from the table and his skateboard from under it.

"What's that for?" Lauren asked.

Josh shrugged. "I never go anywhere without it."

And so they bundled out of the house on Dock Street – Josh on his skateboard and the puppies in the lead, with the girls close behind. Together they sprinted across the massive bridge, heading for the shining towers of Sleuth City.

Big men in dark glasses strode across the wide marble entrance hall of Jimmi D's tower block.

"Stand back," they warned the crowd of reporters and photographers who had waited all morning for a glimpse of the rock star.

Caitlin, Lauren, Megan and Josh arrived just in time to see Jimmi and Helen make a grand exit into a waiting limousine. He was dressed in a bright shirt and jeans. She wore tight black trousers and a shiny red jacket. Her eyes were hidden behind big sunglasses.

"Jimmi!" voices cried. "How do you feel about Tom Drake's arrest?"

For once, the haughty star didn't avoid

the cameras. In fact, he took a detour and left Helen hovering by the car. "I'm glad they locked Drake up," he said, staring into the lenses. "The guy worked for me for ten whole years, and look what he does to repay me!"

"Did you put the cops on to him?"

Jimmi frowned. "It's well known what's been happening in Drake's life recently. He's a mess. The whole world knows he has a giant chip

on his shoulder."

"Are you sure they got the right man?" another reporter yelled. Lights flashed and cameras recorded.

Jimmi D paused for effect. "The police found Drake's fingerprints all over my apartment," he told the reporters. "He'd been at the scene and he had the motive. What more can I say?"

"Jimmi, Jimmi, look this way! Over here!"

Desperate photographers pushed and shoved as the star turned away.

Too late – Jimmi was already in the car. Bodyguards slammed the car doors shut. In an instant Jimmi and Helen were gone.

CHAPTER TEN

There was a rush of photographers down the
street as Jimmi's car drove away. The girls and
Josh used the confusion to slip into the tower
block, where they headed straight for the lift.

"Hold on there!" a girl at the reception desk
cried when she spotted three girls, one
skateboarder and three puppies sprinting
across the hall.

But Josh pressed the button, the doors
closed and they rose smoothly.

"Our old apartment is off to the left," Josh
told the girls as they stepped out again.

"OK, Dylan, we're using Josh's place to try

73

to get into the Diamonds' apartment," Megan explained.

Quick as a flash, Dylan turned left and trotted ahead.

"Smart pup!" Josh muttered. He went ahead and swiped his card through the machine at the door to his old apartment. The door opened and they stepped inside.

"Wow!" Caitlin was impressed. The apartment was almost as big as the rock star's and still had its amazing modern furniture and lamps. She set Daisy down on the floor.

Straight away Daisy trotted to a big window leading on to a narrow balcony. When Caitlin followed and slid open a section of the window, the little Yorkie headed outside.

"Come back!" As usual, Caitlin was scared of the height. She held her breath and followed dainty Daisy, catching sight of the street way below. "D-D-Daisy, be careful!"

But the pup was sniffing at a glass barrier dividing the Drakes' balcony from the one next door. She found a gap just big enough to squeeze under.

Caitlin saw Daisy's rear end disappear under the screen. "Megan, Lauren – come quick!"

Caitlin was worried about Daisy being on her own. She stood on tiptoe and peered over the screen. "Bring me a chair," she told Josh. "I'm going to use it to climb over."

Now it was Megan and Lauren's turn to give advice.

"Make sure the chair doesn't wobble," Megan warned.

"Don't look down!" Lauren told her, as first Caitlin then Josh climbed over the glass screen.

Gingerly, Caitlin lowered herself on to the Diamonds' balcony. Straight away she saw that the rock star's sliding glass door was partly open and that Daisy was already sniffing around the apartment. "We're going in!" she called to Megan and Lauren as Josh rolled his board under the screen and followed her on to the Diamonds' balcony.

"Follow me," Josh told Caitlin. "I know my way around."

"So does Daisy. She's headed straight for the answer machine. It looks like she wants us to play the messages."

Bright-eyed Daisy yapped as Caitlin went across to the phone. She grew more excited

when Caitlin pressed the 'Play Messages' button.

"These pups are amazing!" Josh muttered with a quick shake of his head.

"Shh!" Caitlin warned as the machine clicked and played.

"You have two new messages ... First message received yesterday at 9am."

Josh and Caitlin listened to a woman droning on about not being able to come in and do the housekeeping. *Skip*. Caitlin pressed the button.

"What's going on in there?" Lauren called

from next door. She was on the point of climbing on the chair to follow Caitlin and Josh.

"Wait a sec!" Caitlin listened to the second message.

"Message received yesterday at 2pm . . . Hello Jimmi, this is Tom Drake."

"Yip!" Daisy knew she'd hit the jackpot. *Listen to this!*

"Pick up the phone, Jimmi," Tom Drake's voice insisted. "If you won't talk to me, I'll have to come over personally. We need to talk things through. I've got a good lawyer behind me now. If you don't make the payment, I'll drag you to court and make you cough up. You hear me, Jimmi? I'm on my way!"

The message ended and Josh sat down hard on the nearest couch, close to the fireplace and the big gap on the wall where the Rosier painting should have hung.

"Dad was here," he muttered.

Caitlin nodded. "Which is why the police found lots of fingerprints."

"But it doesn't mean he's guilty," Josh argued.

Caitlin agreed. "Only that he and Jimmi had another argument."

"What's happening?" Lauren asked again. "Let's climb over and join them," she hissed at Megan.

"No, wait." Through the open door of the Drakes' old apartment Megan had heard the *ding!* of the lift and the *swish!* of the door opening. "Someone's coming!" she whispered. "The footsteps are heading towards Jimmi's place."

"Who is it?" Lauren hissed.

Megan peered around the door and saw the back view of a woman wearing a red jacket and black trousers. "It's Helen!" she gasped. "She must have changed her mind about going out. Tell Josh and Caitlin – quick!"

"Watch out – Helen's coming!" Lauren called over the screen.

With a gasp, Caitlin grabbed Daisy and dragged Josh behind the sofa and under the bookcase.

Then Helen came into the apartment. She flung her handbag down on the floor and kicked off her shoes. Then she flicked on the TV. "I'm sick and tired of this nonsense!" she groaned to

herself. "Sick of the photographers, sick of the lies."

"Sshh, Daisy!" Caitlin warned. She was having trouble holding on to her pup.

"Sick of Jimmi!" Helen sighed, as if admitting something which she'd been storing up for a long time. She flopped on to the sofa near the bookcase.

"Yip-yip!" At last Daisy broke free and scampered out from her hiding place.

Helen saw the Yorkie pup and sat up straight. "Where did you come from?" She jumped up to look behind the sofa.

In a panic Caitlin fumbled for the switch that would open the secret door. But Helen had seen them. "OK, stop right there!" she ordered. "Josh? How on earth did you get into this apartment?"

CHAPTER ELEVEN

"Helen, it's not what you think!" Josh emerged from under the bookcase.

"W-w-we were trying to catch Daisy!" Caitlin stammered.

"Yip-yip-yip!" Daisy jumped up on to the sofa and wagged her short tail.

"Yes! Daisy crawled under the screen on the balcony." Josh latched on to Caitlin's excuse. But he knew they were in deep trouble.

Helen's hand hovered over the phone. "I ought to call Security," she muttered. "I mean – what were you doing in your old apartment in the first place?"

"Just picking up a couple of things I forgot when we moved out."

Helen looked him straight in the eye. "That sounds pretty lame to me, Josh. How about telling me the truth?"

"Helen Diamond doesn't believe their story." From behind the balcony screen Lauren could hear every word. "She's going to call Security!"

"Quick, get down from the chair," Megan hissed.

Lauren jumped down and they backed off into the Drakes' old apartment. Dylan and Buster sat quietly, listening and waiting.

"Daisy gave them away!" Lauren could scarcely believe it. "Caitlin's in deep trouble. We should have been there with her!"

"I know. I wish we'd stuck together," Megan agreed. "The Puppy Club shouldn't split up – not ever!"

As the girls sighed and fretted, Dylan and

Buster trotted into the kitchen at the back of the apartment. They took a quick look around then Buster ran to Lauren and jumped up.

"What?" she asked with a frown. "I can't play right now."

Buster bounded off towards the kitchen.

"He wants us to follow," Megan decided.

So they joined the pups, following them to the window and looking out on to the fire escape.

"You want us to go out there?" Megan asked Dylan doubtfully.

The little black Labrador wagged his tail. As Megan unlatched the window, he squeezed out on to the metal staircase with Buster close behind.

"Yep, they definitely

want us to follow," Lauren decided, stepping out after them.

"Wait for me. I'm coming!" Megan cried, stepping out to begin the long climb up to the roof.

"OK, the truth is, we were trying to help Dad." The excuses hadn't worked so Josh came clean with Helen.

"By breaking into our apartment?" she asked.

"I know – it looks bad," Josh confessed. "But I have to work out what happened, for Dad's sake. And Caitlin wants to help."

Quickly Caitlin nodded. "We heard a message on your answer machine," she explained. "We know Josh's dad came to see Jimmi."

"Whoa, I don't need to hear this!" Helen interrupted. "Listen, if Jimmi knew you were here and I was listening to your story, he'd kill me!"

"But he isn't," Josh said.

"And you are," Caitlin added quietly. "I mean – listening. You don't really believe Tom Drake stole your painting either."

A look of alarm flickered across Helen's face. She turned on Caitlin. "What are you saying?"

"It wasn't Tom. He was at home all night with Josh. All he did was come here in broad daylight to get the money Jimmi owes him."

"Yip!" Daisy said from her cushion on the sofa.

"Listen here, Little Miss Know-It-All, you just went a step too far!" Suddenly angry, Helen picked up the phone and spoke into it. "Security? This is Helen Diamond…"

"No, don't!" Josh pleaded. "You're Dad's friend. He wouldn't steal from you and Jimmi. You know that as well as I do!"

Up on the roof, Lauren and Megan followed Buster and Dylan between the satellite dishes and water tanks. Dylan's nose was to the ground, sniffing up every scent. Buster was jumping up at the tall water tanks, snuffling and scurrying from one to another.

"I wish we knew what they were looking for." Feeling helpless, Lauren glanced up at the sky and saw a helicopter drawing near. Its blades whirred noisily as it hovered overhead.

"Watch out – it's going to land!" Megan ran to pick Dylan up and crouch down behind one of the tanks.

"Just our luck!" Lauren groaned. She and Buster joined Megan and Dylan behind the tank.

Sure enough, the helicopter dropped slowly from the sky, its blades churning and sending a wild windstorm across the roof. It landed in the yellow circle and the engine died. Slowly the blades stopped turning and a figure stepped out of the cockpit.

From their hiding place, Megan and Lauren recognised the burly security guard who had chased them with his beefy dog. The dog was

there too, bounding down from the cockpit and sticking close to the security guard's heels.

Megan and Lauren ducked down low and prayed that they wouldn't be seen.

The man reached the entrance to Jimmi Diamond's lift. He'd pressed the button and was about to step inside when he changed his mind, as if he'd forgotten something. Telling his dog to sit, he strode back across the roof.

"Hello, Security? Forget what I just said." Helen gave into Josh's pleas. "I don't need you right now. OK, thanks."

Caitlin breathed a sigh of relief and sat down beside Daisy on the sofa.

Helen took Josh over to the fireplace. Together they stared up at the dark red space where the painting of Fifi and Pierrot the dog once hung. "I never even liked the picture," she confessed. "Neither did Jimmi."

"Dad didn't steal it," Josh insisted more calmly.

There was a long silence then Helen murmured, "I know."

Caitlin gasped. *Let Josh do the talking,* she told herself.

"Why did Jimmi want to make it look like Dad was guilty?" he asked.

Still staring at the space on the wall, Helen gave her answer. "He set Tom up so he wouldn't have to pay him the money he owes. End of story."

Josh nodded but said nothing.

"I went along with it," Helen admitted. "I knew what Jimmi was up to when he pointed the finger at your dad, but I didn't speak out. I mean, you don't argue with Jimmi, ever…"

"I get you," Josh said quietly.

"…But I feel bad," Helen went on. "I don't want Tom to go to jail for something he didn't do."

That was it – Caitlin couldn't sit in silence any more. "So if Tom didn't do it, we have to find out who did!"

Helen shot Caitlin a troubled look.

"There's a real thief out there and he's about to go free unless we do something to stop it."

Caitlin needed to move things on. "You have to tell Jimmi to let Tom Drake off the hook."

Helen looked scared. "I can't."

"Yes you can," Caitlin argued.

"You don't know what you're asking." Helen paced the floor, glancing at Josh then shaking her head.

"There is a way I can help," she said at last. "But you must promise never to tell Jimmi what I'm about to do!"

"Promise!" Josh nodded.

Helen took a deep breath. "OK, come with me."

CHAPTER TWELVE

"Keep your head down!" Megan warned Lauren.

"It is down!" Lauren hissed back.

They could hear Jimmi D's security guard walk to the helicopter, then there was silence except for the wind blowing across the high rooftop.

"Uh-oh!" Lauren craned her neck to see the heavyweight dog squatting by the entrance to the lift. "If we can see him…"

"…He can see us!" Megan gasped at the moment the dog spied them.

With a fierce snarl he galloped towards

them. They could make out his sharp teeth and pink tongue, his mean little eyes.

It was time for Dylan and Buster to act. They leapt out from behind the water tank and stood in front of the cowering girls, challenging the big dog to a fight.

"Poor things – they'll get mashed!" Lauren cried with a loud gasp.

"I can't bear to look!" Megan agreed.

But the little pups were brave. They stood their ground, even when the security guard spotted what was going on.

"Go get 'em, boy!" the security guard yelled. He too raced towards the tall, square tank.

Just then, the lift door opened and Helen stepped out. She took in the scene and turned pale, wheeling round and bumping into Josh,

Caitlin and Daisy as they followed her out through the door.

"Sorry, I can't help you after all," Helen muttered, blindly pushing her way into the lift.

"Come back!" Josh pleaded.

Swish! – the door was closing, stranding Josh, Caitlin and Daisy on the roof.

"What were you going to show us?" Caitlin cried.

"Nothing. I'm sorry." The door shut and Helen was gone.

"OK, first I'll trap the dog!" Lauren decided. She saw a wheelie bin shoved into a dark corner and dragged it out, quickly tipping it on its side.

"While the rest of us deal with the security guard," Megan said firmly.

OK, so he was pretty scary, but he was only one man against three kids. Megan snatched Josh's skateboard and rolled it along the roof, right across the security guard's path.

Back across the roof, Daisy raced to join Dylan and Buster. They stood in line,

daring the guard dog to attack. Meanwhile, Lauren set the upturned wheelie bin in position. "OK, ready!" she hissed.

The guard dog snarled and leapt. At the very last second, the puppies dodged to one side. The dog missed his target. Thrown off-balance he went crashing and screeching like an out-of-control car – right inside the bin.

"Yip-yap!" the puppies cheered as Lauren stood the bin upright and slammed down the lid.

In the chaos, the security guard hadn't seen the skateboard. He stepped right on to it and went sliding out of control. He threw his arms up in the air, yelled when he saw he was heading straight towards the fire escape and yelled again as he disappeared over the edge.

Bump-bump-bump! Megan, Caitlin and Josh heard the heavy man fall from step to step. Then there was silence. "Ouch!" they cringed.

"Don't just stand there – give me a hand!" Lauren insisted.

Inside the bin, the guard dog was barking and head–butting the lid.

So Josh sprinted to help her wheel the bin back into its corner, jamming the lid firmly under a ledge.

"Good job!" Josh grinned, giving Lauren a high five.

But now Dylan, Buster and Daisy set up a chorus of barks. They were trying to scramble up the metal rungs of a ladder bolted to the water tank.

Caitlin reached them first. She stared up at the top of the ladder, steadying her nerves to climb up and see what was inside the tank.

"I'll go!" Lauren cried, dashing to join her.

"No, let me!" Megan too was there in a flash.

But in the end it was Josh who climbed the ladder. "It's my dad who's in trouble," he pointed out. "This is down to me!"

He climbed steadily – one rung, two, then three…

"Hurry!" the girls pleaded, in case the security guard showed up again. From inside the bin, his mad dog whined and yelped.

"What can you see?" Caitlin called as Josh made it to the top.

He peered inside the tank. "It's empty," he reported. "I don't see anything."

"Look again!" Megan told him.

"No – yes, wait!"

"What is it?" Lauren urged.

"There's an object wedged in there – no, I can't reach it!" Josh struggled to feel inside the tank with his fingertips. He made out a flat, square shape, securely taped to the side of the tank. Hitching himself over the rim, he managed to loosen the tape.

"He's going to fall in!" Caitlin bit her lip.

"Got it!" Josh's voice was muffled and hollow. With one final effort he heaved the parcel out of the tank.

"Bring it down! Steady! Watch how you go!"

Caitlin, Lauren and Megan watched Josh's every move.

At last he was back on the ground. He handed over the heavy parcel. The girls tore it open.

And there, still in its gold frame, undamaged and perfect in every way, was a painting of a woman with a black and white dog!

"Case solved!" Megan announced.

CHAPTER TWELVE

The girls and the pups were back in Josh's homely kitchen on Dock Street. Tom Drake was out of jail and Josh's mum, Lucy, was making everyone hot chocolate with marshmallows. Lauren held Buster on her lap. "It turns out *no one* stole the painting. It was a big set up by Jimmi D himself!"

"A dirty trick," Caitlin confirmed. "He took the picture down from the wall and got his security guard to stick it inside the empty water tank. Then he called the police and said it had been stolen."

"No wonder Jimmi and Helen didn't act like they'd been burgled when we first got there," Megan reflected.

"Yeah, and no wonder Helen felt bad when she saw Josh." Sipping hot chocolate, Lauren gave herself a foamy white moustache.

"Framed!" Tom Drake sighed as he sat by Josh. He was an older version of his son – the same floppy fair hair, the same grey eyes.

"It was a neat plan – it could have worked!"

"Yeah, and you'd be in jail for something you hadn't done, and we'd never have got the money Jimmi owes us." Looking ahead, Josh happily pictured the family moving back to a swish apartment once everything was sorted.

"What'll happen to the painting now?" Megan asked.

They'd called the cops and handed the painting over to Agent Greene on the roof of the tower block. Greene had found the security guard unconscious on the fire escape. He'd arrested him on the spot. Jimmi had been picked up soon after in a flash restaurant in central Sleuth City.

'Jimmi D Frames Ex–Manager – The Full Story!' The night's headlines would tell the world the truth.

"I heard Jimmi will probably have to sell it to raise the money he owes me," Tom told

Megan. "And by rights he should end up spending time in jail."

"Thanks to the pups," Megan said with a smile. She finished her chocolate and called Dylan. "They had the whole thing worked out, right from the start."

"And now it's time to go," Lauren said, standing up.

Josh scraped his chair back from the table. "We didn't say thanks yet."

"Thank Buster," Lauren grinned. "And Daisy and Dylan."

"Yip–yap–woof!" The Mystery Pups made it clear that they were happy they'd been able to help.

Standing beside the wide grey river, under the tall yellow cranes of the dockside, Caitlin, Lauren and Megan made the puppies sit in a row.

Quietly Caitlin took a tissue from her pocket and wiped away a tear.

Lauren shot her a puzzled look, until Megan explained. "It's 'cos she said goodbye to Josh!"

"Oh!" Now Lauren got it. Caitlin and Josh – they'd really liked each other.

Caitlin heard Megan whispering. "It's not what you think," she sniffed.

"Yes, it is!" Lauren and Megan said.

Caitlin blinked. "OK, it is," she admitted. She would miss Josh, but right now the three members of the Puppy Club had to work

together to get back home. "I'm OK," she insisted, stuffing the tissue back in her pocket.

So the girls knelt on the quiet dockside and faced Dylan, Daisy and Buster.

"Ready?" Megan asked the pups.

Their eyes twinkled and their ears were pricked.

"Ready?" Lauren asked Caitlin and Megan.

They nodded and all three leant forward to lift the pups' medallions over their heads.

The flat dockside seemed to tilt. The swirling water made them dizzy.

"Whoo!" Lauren cried as the long cranes whirled overhead. "Hang on – here we go!"

And the distant towers of Sleuth City began to fade as the girls and the pups rose high into the sky, through a swirl of grey clouds into clear blue and beyond.

Read more adventures in the

Mystery Pups

series

**Three adorable pups.
One big mystery!**

DOGNAPPED!

A missing pooch, a mystery text message, and a
tearful little rich girl – what on earth is going on in
Sleuth City? The Mystery Pups are about to find out!

978-1-84738-224-5 £4.99

And coming soon...

 ## MISSING!

The feline star of a major movie is missing!
If the Mystery Pups don't find the famous
kitty in time, there's going to be trouble...

978-1-84738-226-9 £4.99

Mystery Pups

This card certifies that

----

is a member of the
Magic Mountain Puppy Club
with his/her puppy

Photo Here